Miniscule

Puny

Dinky

People

For Paulette & November

SIMON & SCHUSTER BOOKS FOR YOUNG READERS
An imprint of Simon & Schuster Children's Publishing Division
1230 Avenue of the Americas, New York, New York 10020
Copyright © 1999 by Peter Selgin

SIMON & SCHUSTER BOOKS FOR YOUNG READERS is a trademark of Simon & Schuster.
Book design by Peter Selgin with Jennifer Reyes
The text for this book is set in Ad Lib ICG.
The illustrations are rendered in gouache.
Printed in Hong Kong
First Edition
10 9 8 7 6 5 4 3 2 1

Library of Congress Cataloging-in-Publication Data
Selgin, Peter.
The "S.S." Gigantic across the Atlantic : the story of the world's biggest
ocean liner ever / Peter Selgin — 1st ed.   p.   cm.
Summary: Tells the tale of the "S.S." Gigantic which began to sink on its maiden
voyage after its rubber hull was punctured by a dreaded sea thumbtack.
ISBN 0-689-82467-X
[1. Ocean liners—Fiction. 2. Shipwrecks—Fiction. 3. Tall tales.] I.Title.
PZ7.S456924Sat 1999 [Fic]—dc21   98-29758   CIP   AC

first
edition

"S.S." GIGANTIC Across the ATLANTIC

The Story of the World's Biggest Ocean Liner Ever!*

and its DISASTROUS maiden voyage

*based on a
true story**
**(sort of)

BY **Peter Selgin**

Simon & Schuster Books for Young Readers

Call me PIP-SQUEAK (everyone else does). Many years ago (never mind how long exactly) I set out to sea on the Biggest Ocean Liner Ever!

I was a mere lad when I first laid eyes on her, rising like a Giant Ghost over the factories, churches, and chimneys of HYPERBOLE, on the Coast of Ireland. . . .

Oh, she was a Beautiful Sight....

GANTiC

Soon as I saw her, I knew
I'd do Anything to sail on her!

Sailors and seamen were gathered around a Captain with a **Big White Beard**. He was saying:

His name was **Captain Bragg**. He was talking about the **Gigantic Ship** I'd seen!

"It's **SO** gigantic, you can't fit it in a picture!"

"It's **SO** gigantic, if you started out as a little boy at the bow of the ship, by the time you walked to the stern you would be a very old man!"

"It's **SO** gigantic, it can travel around the world without moving!"

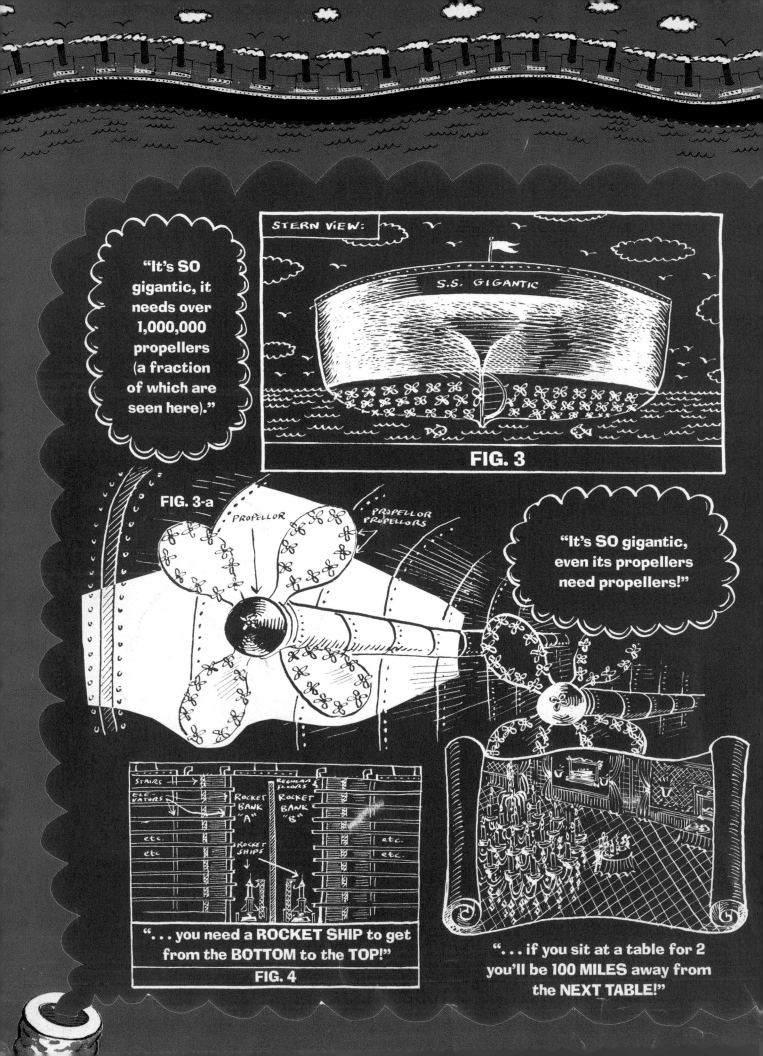

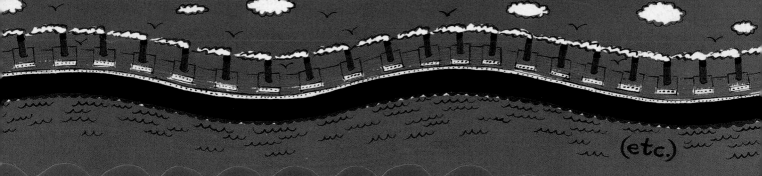

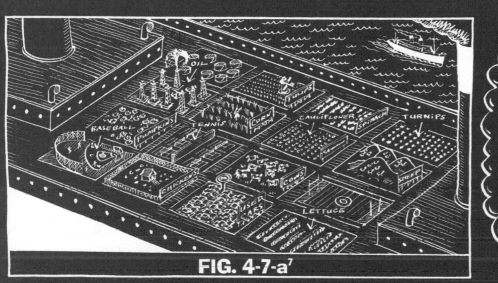

FIG. 4-7-a⁷

"It's **SO** gigantic, it has fields for corn, cows, and baseball! It even has oil fields!"

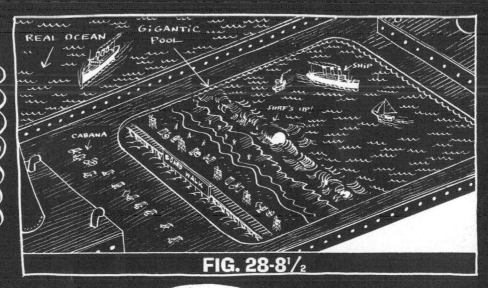

FIG. 28-8¹⁄₂

"It's **SO** gigantic, its pool has a beach and tides and room for other ships!"

"... you need a **MAGNIFYING GLASS** to see the people (or maybe a **TELESCOPE**)."

FIG. 76 ÷ π

"... when it leaves a city the city closes down because there's **NOBODY LEFT!**"

(etc.)

"On my Gigantic Ship, a pip-squeak
like you?" (See what I mean?)
I said, "I'll be your lookout! I can see
better than any of you!"

From across the room I read one of Captain Bragg's uniform buttons. It said: "By Appointment to His Majesty . . . King George III, Button Manufacturers Clyde Q. Cromwell Sons, LTD, Surrey, England. Patent # 0367946-332-01."

Captain Bragg said,

"YOU'RE HIRED!"

And that's how I became the "S.S." GIGANTIC'S lookout!

Diamonds

Gold

One week later, the "S.S." GIGANTIC set off on her Maiden Voyage. The rich passengers were So rich, Giant Cranes were needed to load their Diamonds and Gold!

On "S.S." GIGANTIC'S passenger list that day were (among others):

1

2

3

4

5

6

1. John Jacob Astounding, III

2. J. Pierrepont Pompous
   (BILLIONAIRE FINANCIER)

3. Xavier Extreme
   Exaggerate
   ("S.S." GIGANTIC DESIGNER)

4. Colonel & Mrs.
   Arnchubald Grandeur

5. Benjamin Bigbehind
   (TYCOON)

6. Dr. & Mrs.
   Iadore Myself

...Billionaires, ALL!

As we sailed away, every (little) ship and boat tried to follow us. . . .

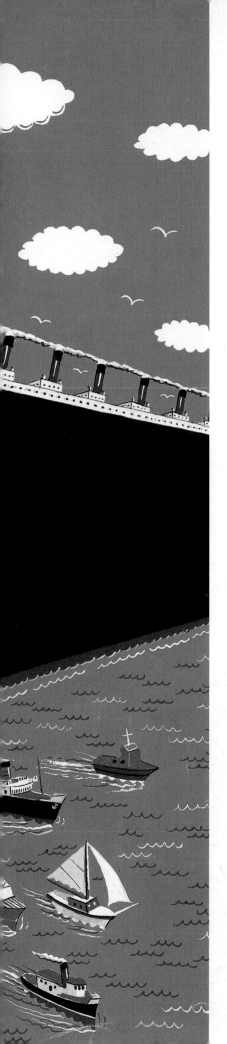

The Billionaire Passengers laughed, danced, and Stuffed their Faces. . . .

Meanwhile, high up in the crow's nest, I kept lookout. . . .

That month, the sea was full of Icebergs. . . .

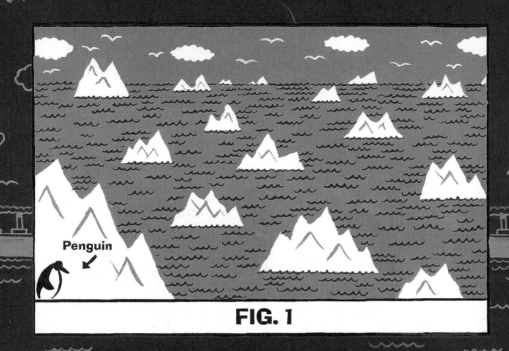

Penguin

FIG. 1

As a result, there were many Sinkings.

Ditto

FIG. 2

As gigantic as
the "S.S." GIGANTIC was,
the average iceberg was
Even More Gigantic!
And yet, the biggest part
was UNDER WATER!

I tried to warn Captain Bragg. "Silly Pip-Squeak," he said. "The 'S.S.' GIGANTIC is unsinkable! It has a Quadruple Hull, and 4,237,864 Watertight Doors! It's SO gigantic it can hold all the water in the world!"*

*(SEE FIG. BX3-470-1.4)

"Besides . . . the 'S.S.' GIGANTIC is made of 100 percent Inflatable, Vulcanized, Waterproof RUBBER!"

FIG. BX3-470-1.4

... I got lost!

I yelled,

"ICEBERG, DEADAHEAD!"

Then I rang my bell.

DiNG! DiNG! DiNG!

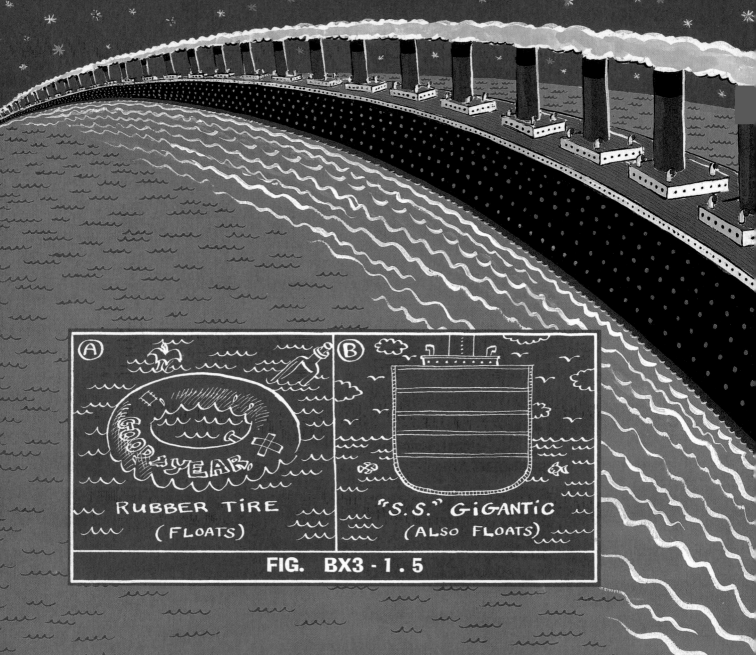

FIG. BX3 - 1.5

A — RUBBER TIRE (FLOATS)

B — "S.S." GIGANTIC (ALSO FLOATS)

. . . But it was **Too Late!** The **"S.S."** GIGANTIC'S waterproof, rubber, quadruple hull **crashed** right into the iceberg, smashing it into a zillion tiny **Ice cubes!** . . .

"See?" said Captain Bragg.
"I told you the 'S.S.' GIGANTIC
is Unsinkable!"

"Maybe so, but (as any good sailor knows)
the ocean contains
Many Mysteries . . . .

DAVY JONES LOCKER

ELECTROLUX

. . . Sea horses, sea urchins,
sea anemones . . . sea snakes,
sea cucumbers, seasaws,
sea vacuum cleaners, and
sea gumball machines
. . . And, most   and
          of All . . .

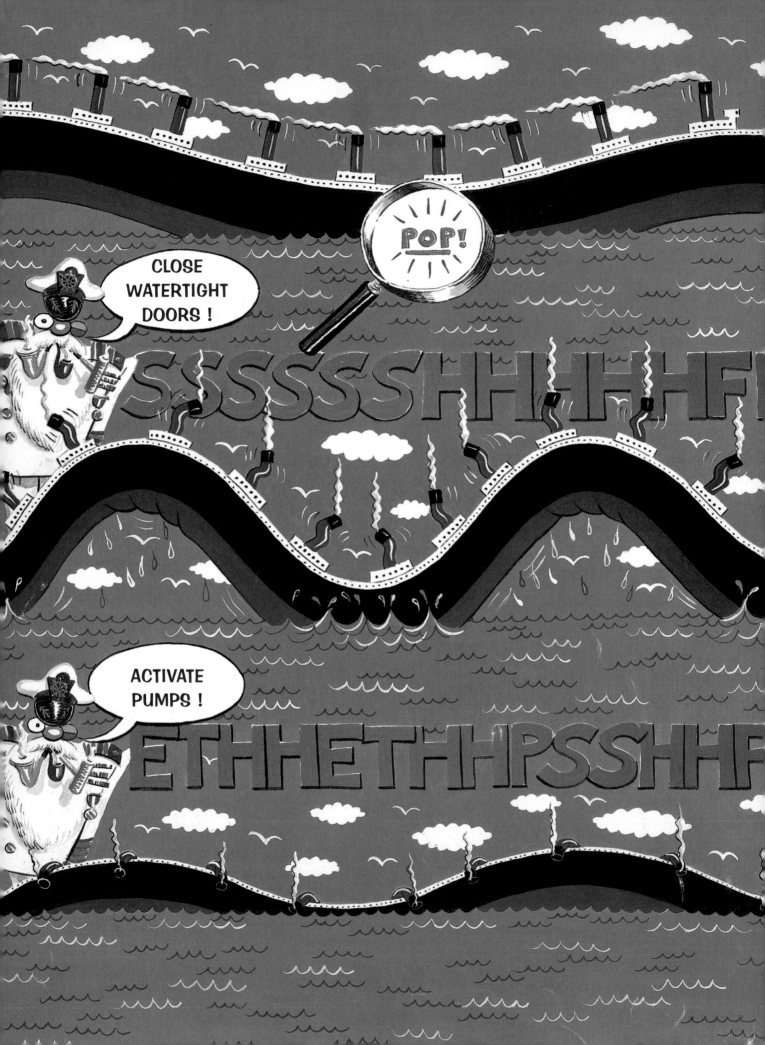

Everyone jumped Overboard.

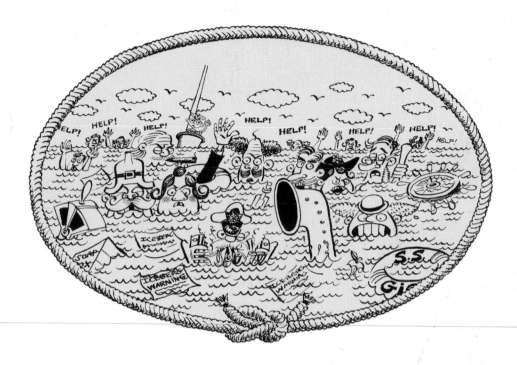

We were all Drowning.

At last, Captain Bragg gave up.

Lucky for us, all the teeny, tiny, miniscule, dinky, bitsy, unimportant, insignificant, pip-squeaky little ships and boats came to the rescue. . . . They saved everyone. . . .

Including Captain Bragg, who got rescued by the itsiest, bitsiest, dinkiest, puniest, weeniest little boat of them All!

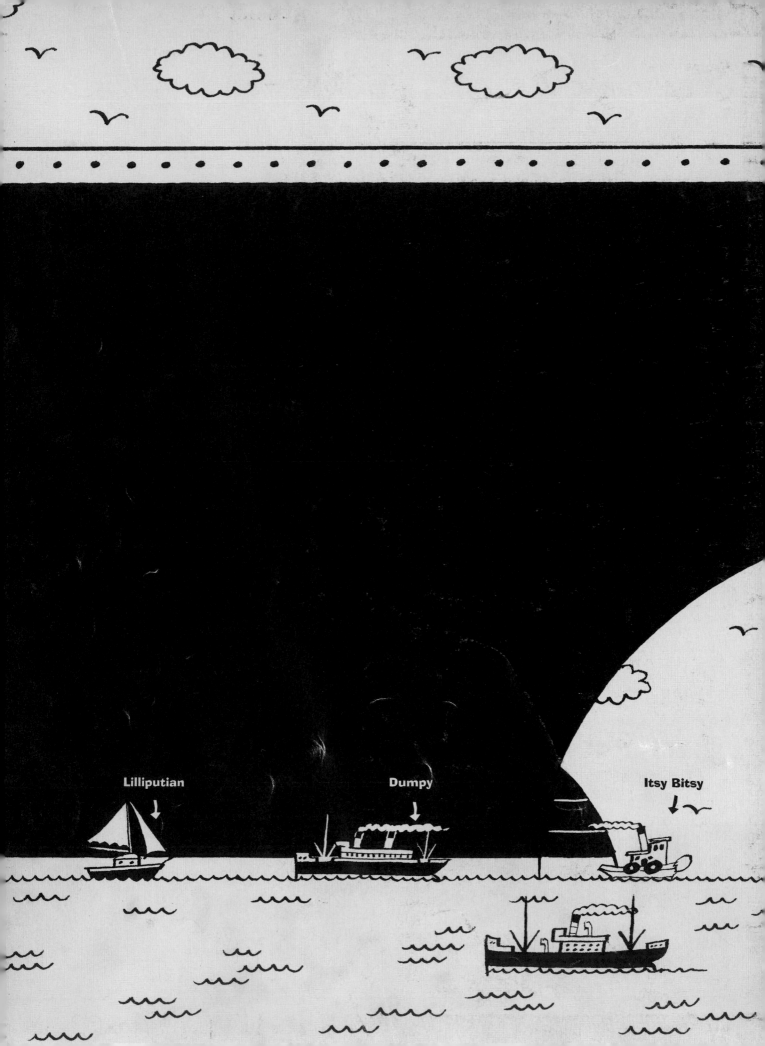

Lilliputian

Dumpy

Itsy Bitsy